For Lissa and Lynn —D. U.

For all the teachers who encouraged
me to be myself —T. L. M.

Henry Holt and Company, *Publishers since 1866*
Henry Holt® is a registered trademark of Macmillan Publishing Group, LLC
175 Fifth Avenue, New York, NY 10010 • mackids.com

Text copyright © 2019 by Deborah Underwood
Illustrations copyright © 2019 by Trenton McBeath
All rights reserved.

ISBN 978-1-250-15176-6
Library of Congress Control Number 2018956062

Our books may be purchased in bulk for promotional, educational, or business use.
Please contact your local bookseller or the Macmillan Corporate and Premium Sales Department
at (800) 221-7945 ext. 5442 or by email at MacmillanSpecialMarkets@macmillan.com.

First edition, 2019 / Design by Sophie Erb
The illustrations in this book were made with graphite pencils, Adobe Photoshop, and sweaters.
Printed in China by RR Donnelley Asia Printing Solutions Ltd.,
Dongguan City, Guangdong Province

1 3 5 7 9 10 8 6 4 2

Ogilvy

illustrations by

Deborah Underwood   T. L. McBeth

GODWINBOOKS

Henry Holt and Company • New York

Ogilvy happily hopped up and down.
The very first day in a very new town!

"I'll zip to the park that I found down the street.
What do they play there? Whom might I meet?"

Bunnies were drawing and knitting and climbing.
A ball game was starting! What wonderful timing!
A great big grin spread across Ogilvy's face.
"I love **ALL** those things! What a marvelous place!"

Ogilvy entered—but why all the staring?

A bunny bounced over. "What *is* that you're wearing?"
Ogilvy paused and looked down at the clothes.

"I'm wearing the thing that I wear, I suppose."

"But is it a sweater or is it a dress?"

"It matters?"
asked Ogilvy.

"Goodness!
Oh, yes!

For bunnies in dresses play ball and knit socks,
and bunnies in sweaters make art and climb rocks."

Ogilvy boggled. "Excuse me, but why?"
"That's just how it is," was the bunny's reply.

"If this is a sweater, I can't throw a ball?"
The bunny said, "No! That would not do at all."

But ball was what Ogilvy wanted to play.

"Then I guess it's a dress.
(Well, at least for today!)"

Outfielder Ogilvy hit a home run

and waved to new friends
when the ball game was done.

The next morning, Ogilvy, wanting to draw,
sat in the park with a pen in a paw.

"But bunnies in dresses don't draw! You know better!"
So Ogilvy answered, "Then this is a sweater."

The next morning, Ogilvy wanted to knit.

"I'll say it's a dress so they won't have a fit."

The *next* morning, Ogilvy wanted to climb

so announced from the rocks,

"It's a sweater this time!"

"What shall I play?" Each day Ogilvy chose,
then decided which name would be best for the clothes.

But some bunnies fumed each time Ogilvy swapped.

They grumbled, "This Ogilvy's got to be stopped!"

So one day as Ogilvy drew on the ground,
a big bunch of bunnies all gathered around.
"Look here," said a bunny, "your garment keeps changing.

We cannot have bunnies who keep rearranging.
So it can be either, but please! Make the call!
A sweater? A dress? Tell us once and for all!"

Now, Ogilvy, just like so many of us,
was not fond of making a ruckus or fuss.

But frustrated, Ogilvy made a hard choice
and took a big breath and found a BIG voice.

"I like to do *all* these things! Why must I hide this?
I just do not see why I need to decide this!

Don't some of you sweater
buns want to knit socks?

Don't some of
you dress-wearers
yearn to climb rocks?

Why are you all so absurdly obsessed?
Why do you care so much how we are dressed?
I'm tired of all of the questions and staring!

I'm wearing an

Ogilvy!

That's what I'm wearing!"

The bunnies fell silent, then halted the fight.
For could it be Ogilvy Bunny was . . . right?

"It really *is* silly for clothes to divide us.

Let's do all the things that till now were denied us!"

So bunnies in sweaters played any old game.
And bunnies in dresses? Precisely the same.

The things they were wearing caused no interference,
and even some ogilvys made an appearance.

One day a new bunny bounced by the brook.
The bunnies all crowded around for a look

at the curious thing on the new bunny's head.
The bunnies all paused, and then . . .

OME!"

they said.

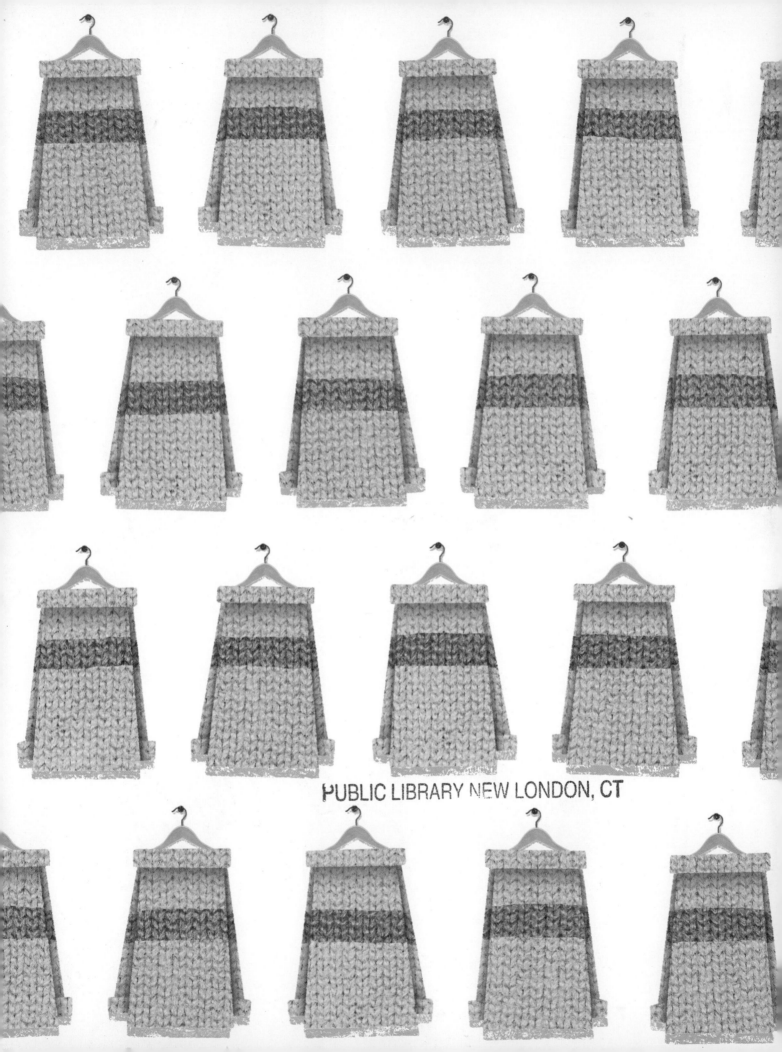